When
Spring Comes
to the DMZ

Published by Plough Publishing House
Walden, New York
Robertsbridge, England
Elsmore, Australia
www.plough.com

비무장지대에 봄이 오면 By Uk-Bae Lee

This English edition is published by arrangement with Sakyejul Publishing Ltd., Paju, Korea.

ISBN: 978-0-87486-972-9
23 22 21 20 19 18   1 2 3 4 5 6

A catalog record for this book is available from the British Library.
Library of Congress Cataloging-in-Publication Data

Names: Lee, Uk-Bae, author, illustrator. | Won, Chungyon, translator. | Won,
   Aileen, translator.
Title: When spring comes to the DMZ / Uk-Bae Lee ; translated from the Korean
   by Chungyon Won and Aileen Won.
Other titles: Bimujang chidae e bom i omyon. English
Description: Walden, New York : Plough Publishing House, [2019] | Summary:
   Grandfather returns each year to the demilitarized zone, the barrier--and
   accidental nature preserve--that separates families that live in North and
   South Korea.
Identifiers: LCCN 2018037211 | ISBN 9780874869729 (hardcover)
Subjects: LCSH: Korean Demilitarized Zone (Korea)--Juvenile fiction. | CYAC:
   Korean Demilitarized Zone (Korea)--Fiction. | Korea--Fiction. |
   Nature--Fiction. | Seasons--Fiction. | Grandfathers--Fiction.
Classification: LCC PZ7.Y525 Wh 2019 | DDC [E]--dc23
LC record available at https://lccn.loc.gov/2018037211

Printed in China

When Spring Comes to the DMZ

Uk-Bae Lee

Translated by Chungyon Won and Aileen Won

Plough Publishing House

When spring comes to the DMZ,
green shoots spring up in the meadows.

But you cannot go there because
the razor wire fence is blocking the way.

When spring comes to the DMZ,
the seal family swims from Bohai Bay
to Baengnyeong Island.
Warships from South Korea and North Korea
face off in the sea near the island,
but the seals come and go freely.

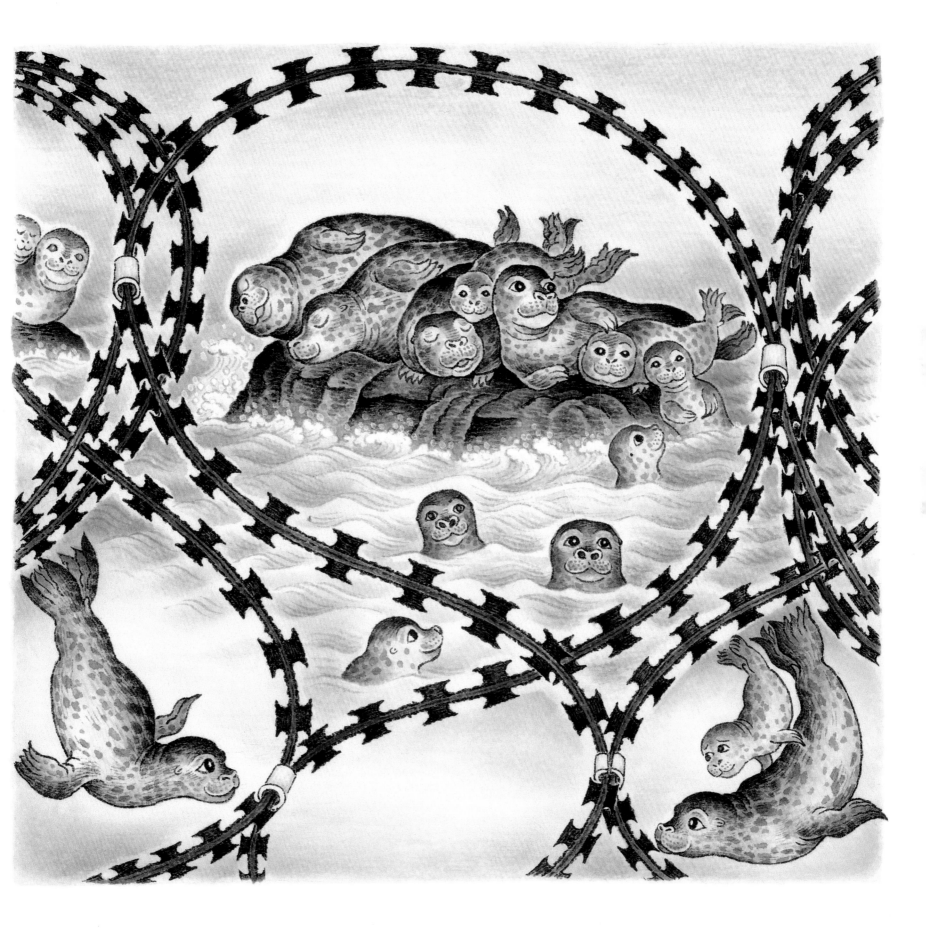

When spring comes to the DMZ,
soldiers check the fence
and fix the broken places.

Grandfather climbs up
to the DMZ observatory
and looks at the northern sky.

When summer comes to the DMZ,
the birds return to the Imjin River.
They build nests, hatch their young,
and make a loving family.

When summer comes to the DMZ,
the otter brothers and sisters
cool off on hot days
by playing in the water,
and the young water deer
nibble on water lily leaves.

When summer comes to the DMZ,
the soldiers march in line
and undergo exhausting training.

Grandfather goes up to the DMZ again
and stares out over the northern land.

When autumn comes to the DMZ,
the salmon from the Pacific Ocean
swim many miles upstream to return
to the place where they were born.
They smell the water of their home,
struggle bravely upstream,
lay their eggs, and so finish their lives.

When autumn comes to the DMZ,
the leaves in Gojindong Valley turn bright colors
and the baby mountain goat
follows its mother,
jumping up the steep mountainside.

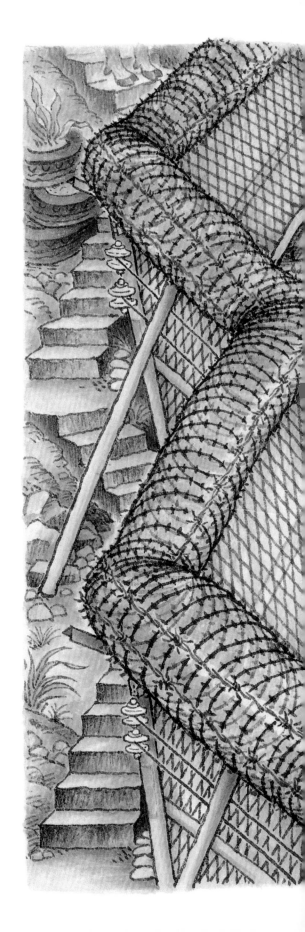

When autumn comes to the DMZ,
the soldiers practice with their tanks and fighter planes.

Grandfather goes to the DMZ once again
and looks at the empty northern sky.

When winter comes to the DMZ,
on the mountains and meadows
and on the fence that divides
the South and the North
the white snow blossoms.

When winter comes to the DMZ,
birds from the north fly south
over the wide Cherwon Plains,
calling out: "Du-ru-ru, du-ru-ru,"
"gwan—, gwan—," "ki-ruk, ki-ruk."

When winter comes to the DMZ,
the soldiers from the South
and the soldiers from the North
look at the round moon and think of their homes.

Grandfather climbs up to the DMZ lookout again
and gazes at the snow-covered northern land.

Grandfather wants to fling the

He wants to walk out
    into the green meadow
        and lie in the sunny grass
            looking up at the blue sky . . .

When spring comes to the DMZ again . . .
Grandfather no longer wants to climb
the stairs to look at the DMZ.

. . . because this is Grandfather's beloved home country.

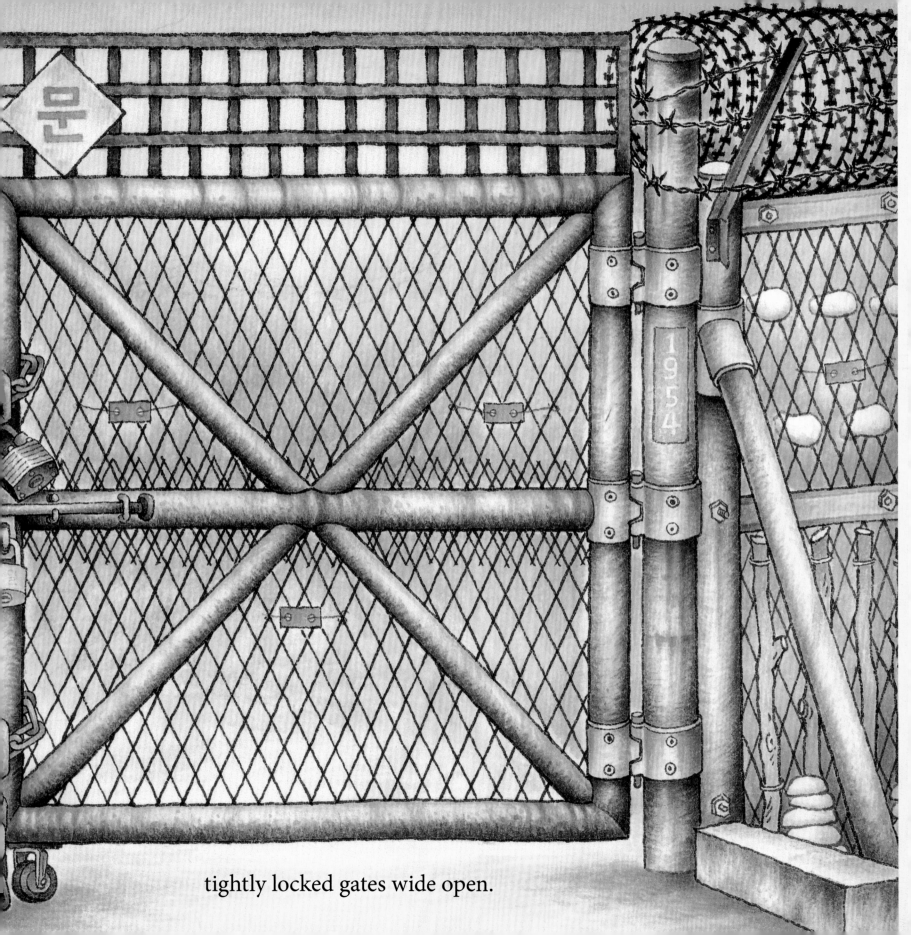

tightly locked gates wide open.

The Korean Peninsula: Two in One

If you look at a map, you'll see that the Korean Peninsula is divided into two countries. It wasn't always that way. The Japanese occupied Korea from 1910 until 1945. At the end of World War II the United States and the Soviet Union liberated Korea from the Japanese and split the country into South and North along the 38th parallel. In 1950 the Korean War broke out between the South and the North. Over the next three years, millions of people were injured or killed, and many families lost their homes. When the war ended with a cease-fire, the dividing line was redrawn. From that time until today, Korea remains divided and many families are still separated and unable to meet freely.

What Is the DMZ?

The truce that ended the Korean War established the border at the Military Demarcation Line where the two armies had stopped fighting. On either side of the line, about one and a quarter miles back, South and North Korea each put up fences. Between these fences lies the demilitarized zone, or DMZ, which stretches 154 miles from the mouth of the Imjin River in the west to Goseong in the east. A demilitarized zone means an area with no weapons, but there are many heavily armed soldiers on both sides, constantly watching each other across the DMZ.

Because people are not allowed to cross into the DMZ, it has become a sanctuary for a wide variety of wildlife that has disappeared or become endangered in other places. As a result, people often call the DMZ a paradise for wildlife. In reality, it is not a paradise but a last refuge.

Turning the DMZ into a Land of Peace

The DMZ is now more than sixty-five years old. Razor wire still scars the hills and valleys, old landmines lie buried there, and both sides bristle with dangerous weapons. The DMZ should be preserved as a wildlife refuge, but it is time to roll away the razor wire, dispose of the landmines, and clear away the weapons. Railways should be reconnected so separated families can meet again. Then Korea can become a land where all life, including humans, can live in peace and freedom.

Uk-Bae Lee was born in Yongin, South Korea, in 1960 and studied art at Hongik University. After school he joined a group of artists who wanted to give the poor a voice. Lee held free painting classes for factory workers. Later, inspired to make a book for his own young daughter, he began writing and illustrating children's books. In 2010 he created *When Spring Comes to the DMZ* in Korean as part of the Peace Picture Book Project by illustrators from Korea, China, and Japan. Since then he has often talked to groups of children and parents about how they can work for peace.